Library of Congress C.I.P. Data
Drescher, Henrik. Look-alikes.   1. Children's
stories, American. [1. Dolls—Fiction]   I. Title.
PZ7.D78383Ru 1985   [E]   85-225
ISBN 0-688-05816-7 ISBN 0-688-05817-5 (lib. bdg.)

for my mother and father
and camilla and Frits and Laurien

special thanks to my editor Barbara lalicki
and everyone at lothrop. lee and shepard
for their patience
and
encouragement

LOOK-ALIKES

HENRIK DRESCHER

LOTHROP, LEE & SHEPARD BOOKS · NEW YORK

The Pearsons lived on an island
on a small green planet in the middle of space.

One morning, Mr. and Mrs. Pearson, their son Rudy,
and Buster the monkey were enjoying breakfast.
Suddenly, Buster babbled in rhyme.

He made mysterious signals to Rudy.

With a jump that sent the dishes flying,
Buster sprang from the porch.

Rudy followed across the lawn . . .

up the tree, and into a secret treehouse.

Inside, they found a box full of toys.
Among them were two familiar-looking dolls.

Rudy and Buster were playing with their look-alikes on a toy island when, suddenly, the toys ran across the lawn, up the tree, and into a secret treehouse.

Peeking through the door, Buster and Rudy
saw a curious red room.

They watched the look-alikes climb a rubber-necked
creature's trunk and disappear through a window.

The dolls' adventure had begun.

They didn't know what was up . . .

"SQUAWK! Get out of my nest!"

"*HELP!*" screamed Buster. "*YIKES!*" yelled Rudy.

SPLASH! They were dropped into a soupy situation.

"Wait for me," cried Buster, and off they galloped.

"Look! An egg."

"This egg is no egg. It's a tunnel."

SWOSH! SPLASH! SLIDE!

"Whoever you are, please get us out of this crazy place!"

And, in a roundabout way, that's just what he did.

Their stomachs tickled and their heads were spinning
when they waved goodbye

Rudy and Buster welcomed their look-alikes back.

Then they returned the dolls to the warm and cozy chest.

Rudy and Buster climbed down the old tree.

The sun was setting as they darted home,
hungry and tired,

into the arms of Mr. and Mrs. Pearson.

Then dinner was served, and this time,
Buster didn't monkey around.

After bathing and brushing their teeth,
they were tucked into bed.

That night Rudy and Buster slept well.

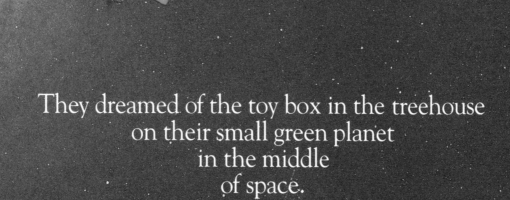

They dreamed of the toy box in the treehouse
on their small green planet
in the middle
of space.